That Tender Light

An Owen Family Novella

Also by Marsha Ward

Gone for a Soldier
The Man from Shenandoah
Spinster's Folly
Ride to Raton
Trail of Storms

Mended by Moonlight

The Zion Trail

That Tender Light

An Owen Family Novella

Marsha Ward

WestWard Books

Payson, Arizona

WestWard Books
P O Box 53
Payson, Arizona 85547
www.westwardbooks.com

Publisher's Note: This is a work of fiction. Names, characters, places, and incidents are a product of the author's imagination. Locales and public names are sometimes used for atmospheric purposes. Any resemblance to actual people, living or dead, or to businesses, companies, events, institutions, or locales is completely coincidental.

Cover Design by Linda Boulanger
www.telltalebookcovers.weebly.com
Book Layout © 2017 BookDesignTemplates.com

That Tender Light / Marsha Ward -- 1st ed.
ISBN 978-1-947306-04-2

Thank you to my beta readers, who did such a stellar, quick job for me: Anna Wilder, Becky Rohner, Betsy Love, Deb Eaton, Debra Erfert, Sheila Summerhays, and Stephanie Abney. Your help is very much appreciated.

CONTENTS

Chapter 1

As she lay dying, Rod Owen's mother made him promise to find a good, Christian woman to marry.

"Mind that she be a church-goer, Roderick, or me and your pa and all the ghostly shades of the Yancey and Owen families, God bless 'em, will haunt you till kingdom come."

Rod had sworn an oath to his mother and held her hand as the life went dark in her feisty eyes. Then, putting aside his deep grief, he bought her the finest funeral he could afford in 1838, and laid her to rest in the Mount Jackson, Virginia, cemetery beside his father, whose stone read, "Rulon Peter Owen, beloved husband and father," along with his birth and death dates.

A year later, he could finally afford a matching stone for "Nellie Marie Yancey Owen, beloved wife and mother," but had not yet found a church-going woman to marry.

Not that he hadn't tried.

He made his first attempt at courting with a fetching girl in Mount Jackson named Muriel Cathy, but he was too late. She only had eyes for the companion of his youth, Chester Bates, and soon married him. Rod could hardly refuse his friend's request that he attend him as his best man. He handed a circle of gold to Chester, and was obliged to observe as the man slipped the ring onto the girl's finger.

Once he had swallowed his pride and disappointment, Rod paid court for some weeks to Rebecca Penewit of Woodstock. The ride on horseback was long, and he wasn't sure how deep the girl's piety sunk into her heart, but she was comely, with yellow hair and blue eyes, much like his own. However, when he tasted the doughy, soggy apple pie she made especially for him, he ceased calling on her as soon as good manners would permit.

There had been other attempts, but he felt no lasting connection with any of the women.

Now, two years after his mother's passing, he rode along the Shenandoah Valley pike toward Front Royal, wondering how much leeway she would allow before she gathered the ghosts to disturb his sleep. He'd done his best to keep his promise, but with no kith or kin to help him on the increasingly prosperous farm outside Mount Jackson, he had little time to go a-courting.

Two days ago, Rod had received a letter from a wealthy young man named Madox who resided in Front Royal, asking him to come discuss a matter of business. A stranger looking at Rod's homestead would say his business was farming, but he would not be completely correct. Above all else, his business was horses. He bred them, trained them, and sold them, and his reputation in the field was spotless. He had learned all he knew from his late father. Someday, he hoped to have sons to teach in the same way he had been taught. But before he could have sons, he must have a wife, and his lack of success in that search pressed dismally upon his soul.

There was no denying he was lonely. He certainly could use a wife around the farmstead, but he resisted the thought of installing just any woman into his home . . . or his bed. He had certain standards besides the one his mother had set, that she be a godly woman.

He knew now that he wanted a slim, raven-haired girl whose apple pie would please his palate, whose wit would spark his intellect, and whose form would weaken his knees and quicken his pulse all the days of his life. She also had to be God-fearing. He didn't know of such a female within a hundred miles of home.

Rod shook his head as he jogged along on the horse. For the present, he should concentrate on whatever business young Madox had for him. Perhaps when he had accomplished that task, he could widen his search for a fitting wife.

~*~*~

Julia Helm wiped the streaming tears off her cheeks, then climbed up onto the wooden spring seat of the farm wagon weathered almost white. Her brother Jonathan's firm hand on her elbow steadied her somewhat, but the overwhelming sadness that had brought the tears remained. She looked at the stone house in the faint light before full dawn, the wooden barn with its wide doors, the early spring fields smelling of molding corn stalks. *Why this sadness? I'll see Cumberland County again in two months.*

Jonathan handed her the small wooden box containing her recipe collection, and she clutched it to her breast. She pulled her brown wool cloak more tightly around her shoulders and wrenched her gaze from the house. Couldn't she simply tell Jonathan she had changed her mind? Tell her brother to unhitch the team of gray horses while she ran back inside the house and into her small, cozy room to curl up in the comfort of Papa's upholstered chair? Cousin Camilla didn't really need her help to prepare for the wedding. Her cousin's father, Uncle Phillip, had plenty of sla— servants who could help. Besides, Virginia was so far away from Pennsylvania. The trip would take two weeks! Two weeks of travel behind the rumps of the big horses, being jostled and jolted until her young bones could hardly stand to travel another yard, let alone another mile. And all for what? Camilla's gratitude? The chance to see Aunt Susannah again?

The wagon groaned and creaked as Jonathan climbed into the wagon seat on the other side, then leaned over to tuck the brown woolen blanket covering her lap under her far knee. "Mind you tell me if you get cold," he said, and grinned at her like a crazy man, his breath clouding around his ruddy face underneath his knitted cap as he lifted the leather lines.

Jonathan loves adventure. Why can't I work up enthusiasm like his?

It was no use. Julia knew she was a homebody. She liked being a homebody. She enjoyed cooking and cleaning and doing for her older brother, creating a calm household for the pair of them, orphans since their father's death three years before. Fortunately, no one had come around when Papa died to tell her that twelve was too tender an age for her to be doing all the work around the house while Jonathan kept the farm going and hired himself out to earn the cash money they needed. He had ten years of age on her, so folks must have figured he could care for himself and his little sister, too.

The horses moved briskly in the chilly morning, trotting along the half-frozen road toward Haldeman's Town. True to her anticipation, the wheels caught every bump and chuckhole in the road, transferring the harsh movement up the axle to the wagon's frame and then to the seat. Even the leaf springs between the wagon box and the seat could not prevent the jolts from acting on her thin posterior. Perhaps if she had a nice cushion of fat on her behind like that of old Mrs. Curry, this trip would not be so distressing.

"Spring is on its way. Can't you smell it?" Jonathan asked.

Julia took a sniff, but didn't think there was anything in the common smells of the farm that indicated a change of seasons. "I don't know what you smell," she said with a shake of her head. "I smell the corn stalks moldering and the horse droppings you just ran the wheels through on purpose to annoy me, but I don't smell spring."

"Ah, is your nose too dainty to pick up the breath of new life?"

Jonathan *would* tease her about her small nose. Tears welled in her eyes again. It was no use asking him to quit. That would only make him find something worse to tease her about. She gripped her recipe box and ran the contents through her mind as she blinked away the tears.

Hash. Flannel cakes. Notes on roasting fowl. Directions for making Indian pudding. Boiled beans. Rabbit stew. Which spice went well with which dish. Apple pie cloaked in the delicate lard pastry Aunt Susannah taught me to make two summers ago. Ginger snap cookies. Now *that* was her best dish. Jonathan didn't joke about her cookies. She would have to make them for Aunt Susannah and Uncle Phillip the first chance she got. Maybe even for the wedding guests. She envisioned tons and tons of ginger snaps, crispy brown circles heaped on silver trays passed around to the guests by servants dressed in white coats that contrasted with their dark skin.

Would Uncle Phillip ever free his slaves?

She doubted it. Uncle Phillip was a pleasant man, but he seemed oblivious to the evil of owning men and women, and even little children. Julia shuddered. The new preacher was quite an abo- abolish- no, abolitionist. His recent sermons had dwelt on the wretched lives of those descended from captured Africans, and the need to make Southerners see the evil of their slave-holding ways.

Does that mean Uncle Phillip is evil?

That wasn't possible. Uncle Phillip had always been so kind to her. She would never be able to think of him as evil.

The rising sun revealed their approach to Haldeman's Town, and Julia breathed a sigh of relief. Jonathan would stop at the mercantile for supplies, and she could get down and walk around before they resumed their journey south.

~*~*~

Rod trotted the sorrel mare around the horse training ring beside his barn, pleased with the progress of the animal in the time it had been under his training. It wouldn't be long before he could deliver the horse to the large Roush place near New Market. William Madox required that he do so before he took the Roush girl as his bride in the early part of May. He yet had a few weeks.

The mare was nearly ready, though. It had been easy to break. It responded to reined commands, had an even gait, and was a good-natured animal. Perhaps he could deliver the horse next week and get about his search for a God-fearing wife.

His friend, Chester, had offered to introduce him to his wife Muriel's older sister. However, the woman was older than he, and Rod didn't want to go in that direction. Somewhere, there must be a girl who would stir his senses, perhaps even as they worshipped together.

Shame on you! He shouldn't mix devotion to God and matters of the, uh, heart.

Finished with the mare for the day, he took it back to the barn and cared for its needs, then entered the house his father had built for his mother when they had wed. Passing through the kitchen door, he remembered how his father had sometimes come in for the night, crept up behind his mother as she worked on supper—unaware that Rod was observing from the parlor—encircled her with his sunburned arms, and planted a kiss under her ear.

Rod brought his hand down flat on the kitchen work table with such force that the wood vibrated in protest under his palm. *I want that. I want a girl I can nuzzle in an odd moment, a girl who won't mind a little lovin' in the kitchen.*

His supper seemed even more solitary than usual that night. But when he opened the Bible in the parlor for his customary devotions before bed, he came upon a verse in the Book of Joshua that served to brighten his mood. Verse nine in chapter one read, *Have not I commanded thee? Be strong and of a good courage; be not afraid, neither be thou dismayed: for the Lord thy God is with thee whithersoever thou goest.*

He closed the book on his finger and looked into the embers glowing on the bed of the brick fireplace his father had built so many years before. Yearning welled up from the depths of his soul, but it didn't have a bitter taste tonight. Undertones of hope swirled through the emotion, comforting him. The Good Lord knew his desires, even the physical ones, and peace joined the tender threads of hope in his heart.

"There *is* a girl for me out there, somewhere," he whispered. "I'm going to find her. I'm going to find her soon."

~*~*~

When Jonathan helped Julia down from the old wagon seat in the yard behind Uncle Phillip's big house, she wanted nothing more than to sleep for a week. But that was not to be, for Cousin Camilla pounced on Julia, dragged her into the house and up the stairs, and spread the end of a bolt of white silk upon her bed.

"Isn't it beautiful, little Julia?" Camilla said, fingering the smooth fabric and cooing on and on about the magnificent dress it would be.

Julia made appropriate responses, wondering why her cousin was not even concerned about whether or not Julia needed to refresh herself after her long journey.

It was really no mystery. Camilla thought of Camilla's welfare before all else. Aunt Susannah, God love her, thought her daughter hung the moon, so with an upbringing of coddling and the granting of every wish, it was no wonder that Julia had to remind her cousin that she needed to relieve herself and wash up before she could discuss wedding plans.

Camilla made a face and said, "Well, of course I know that. Come along. I'll show you where you're to stay."

Camilla was waiting when Julia reappeared in the hallway from her spare, but very adequate lodgings.

"You simply must see the lace for the bodice.

It will overlay the silk. Father bought me the most elegant necklace and earrings to wear. I'm worried that a full veil will hide them, but Mother insists on a trailing veil over the skirt's train." Camilla's mouth twisted, then her face brightened. "I shall have a chance to throw back the front piece of the veil so that William may kiss me after we make our vows. He shall be the first to see the necklace. Oh Julia, I'm going to be the most beautiful bride of the year!"

Despite her exhaustion, Julia endeavored to be enthusiastic for Camilla's sake. After all, a girl would only marry once, and she supposed a girl of Camilla's standing must make a grand show.

"You are to work on the dress," Camilla said.

Julia's horror must have shown on her face, for Camilla continued in a rush, "Oh, I don't mean the cutting and sewing. I know you're not an experienced seamstress. Mrs. Grant will have the majority of the task. *You* will do the hems. You can certainly manage that."

Her cousin's disdain stung, but Julia merely nodded at the scheme. So she was here to do what any servant could accomplish. Camilla probably thought she was bestowing a great honor upon her "little" cousin.

"Of course," she said, straightening her spine and throwing back her shoulders. She would not allow her cousin's attitude of superiority to affect her own outlook, even though she felt off-kilter because she missed her home in Cumberland County so much. *Ah well, I won't be here forever.*

~*~*~

Jonathan left two days later, promising Julia he would return in time for the wedding and their subsequent journey home. As soon as he drove the wagon down the lane toward the Valley Pike, Camilla swooped in and took Julia off to town to shop—accompanied by her driver and maid—and thus Julia began her labors on Camilla's behalf without her beloved brother's presence.

She wasn't treated like a slave. On the contrary, Aunt Susannah and Uncle Phillip greeted her warmly and gave her the same treatment as they did their own children. Aunt Susannah had a new dress made for her, one suitable for Sabbath worship, but serviceable for party-going, as well, for she was included in every occasion, including two pre-wedding parties. At the first, she was introduced to the bridegroom, William Madox, and his family, who had arrived from their homes in Front Royal especially for the festivity. At the second, a celebration with Camilla's friends, Aunt Susannah endeavored to introduce Julia to several young men of the neighborhood, but

Julia was not taken with any of them. She certainly wasn't going to marry a Virginia boy! They had nothing on the men from Cumberland County. She supposed. She hadn't any remarkable acquaintance with any of them, but surely, in time, someone special would appear to court her.

Aside from the two parties, Julia led a quiet life, hemming the voluminous skirt by day, and sleeping restlessly at night, wondering if she were too young to worry about her future.

Chapter 2

Julia sat on the porch, hemming the skirt of Camilla's silk wedding gown and hoping for a cooling breeze to spring up, when she heard the sound of hooves on the lane that came in from the Valley Pike. She glanced up. A man on horseback approached, leading a sorrel horse. He sat erect in the saddle, hat pushed back from his brow so she saw light-colored hair spilling from beneath it. The nearer he came, the better she could discover his features, for the sun shone full upon a strong face. It was long and lean, with pronounced cheekbones and no facial hair. He was younger than she had thought at first glance, but not a youth of her own age. She guessed he was several years older, perhaps Jonathan's age or a few years his junior. Camilla wouldn't call him handsome, but his confident seat in the saddle and the way one golden lock of hair curled forward under his ear made Julia's breath catch in her throat.

Her heartbeat quickened; she could feel it thudding against her ribs and wondered at her reaction. She didn't know the young man. She had not seen him at either of Camilla's parties. She didn't know if he was of a good family, or if he had any money, or if he worshipped God. She only knew that he was going to make a vital change in her life.

Julia tried to swallow, but there was no moisture in her throat. He was gazing at her, quite pointedly, in fact, as he came closer. His blue eyes mesmerized her, holding her captive in their vibrant depths. She feared he could hear the thunder of her heart, feared that it would reveal to him that she could no more look down at the fabric in her lap than she could fly into the nearby trees.

Then he drew rein, stopping his horses, still gazing at her. He removed his hat with the hand holding the lead rope. His mount danced sideways, nearer to her. He took a moment to control it, then met her eyes again. "Good day, miss," he said in a deep voice steeped in Virginia charm. "Are you a God-fearing lady?"

Her throat still parched, she could only nod, and wonder at his question.

He glanced at her hands, frozen over the silken garment. She felt broken until he raised his eyes again and stared into hers. "Not married? No domestic entanglements?"

She shook her head, astonished at his bold questions. Then he seemed to search her very soul with those eyes. Her face warmed. What was he discovering with his steady gaze?

He gave a slight nod, and asked, "You're free to marry me?"

Her hand rose to cover her mouth at the same time all nature paused, took a breath, and then gathered its forces to spill golden light upon the head of the young man waiting for her reply.

Her body, light as air, yearned for his hand to pull her back to earth. Her mind raced over the catalogue of social conventions his words had shattered to bits. *We've never been introduced. I don't know his name. He doesn't know mine. I have no chaperone. I have no dowry. Jonathan is not here to consider his suitability. Does he make enough of a living to support a wife? Does he own slaves? What does he do?*

Even so, the tingling in every nerve told her that this man was unusual, that his words were not spoken lightly, nor in jest. He wasn't mocking her. His direct approach had cut through every impediment, every excuse she could raise due to social custom. Her heart fluttered, a captive moth beating its wings in her bosom.

But one conversation did not a courtship make. Although the strength of his personality tugged at her heart, her head insisted upon making her reply.

Julia cleared her throat. She swallowed, grateful that she now could. She moistened her lips, then she steadied her voice.

"You're welcome to court me," she said, then picked up her needle, looked to her task, and took a stitch in Camilla's hem.

His laughter rolled over her like warm honey. "Spunky," he said, "and well spoken, besides."

She looked up. He cocked his head and grinned at her. She felt her defenses slipping.

"Will you do me the honor of findin' someone to introduce us, just as soon as I deliver this horse?"

She smiled. He wasn't ignorant of society's normal behaviors. He had merely ignored them for some purpose of his own. Aunt Susannah could serve as an intermediary. Or perhaps it would be more proper if Uncle Phillip did that bit of work.

"I will," she replied, and cast her gaze downward, but not before she saw that his grin widened.

"I'll see you again in an hour in the parlor." He tipped his hat to her, set it back on his golden locks, clucked his tongue at the horse, and rode out of her sight toward the back of the house.

Julia put three fingertips to her forehead and filled her lungs with air. Who was that man, and how had he awakened such a multitude of emotions in her? Birds she had never noticed chirped in the bushes lining the porch. A bee flew by, buzzing industriously. A breeze arose and cooled her brow.

She looked at her work. Only three stitches remained for her to do. She finished them as rapidly as she dared, then gathered up the skirt and the sewing basket and hurried into the house. She must hang the gown and then find Uncle Phillip.

She burst into Camilla's room and opened the armoire door. She hung the skirt of the wedding gown next to the bodice and arranged its folds to prevent wrinkles. Someone came into the room behind her. Securing the armoire door closed, Julia turned and met her cousin's eyes, her cheeks burning.

Camilla looked Julia over. "What's going on? Something about you has changed."

Julia thought, *I have met the man I will marry*, but aloud she asked, "Do you know the whereabouts of your father?"

"Father? I saw him go toward the stable. Someone brought him a horse. A Mr. Owen, I think." She opened the armoire and admired her gown, then turned and looked at Julia, furrowing her brow. "What do you want with Father?"

Only to make my life better, she thought. *With Mr. Owen.* She savored the sensation of the name settling deep into the corridors of her mind, then recalled Camilla's query.

"I need to ask him a question."

"I can most probably give you an answer." Camilla arched an eyebrow.

"Not for this," Julia replied, and left as quickly as she could. *Not for this.*

~*~*~

Rod Owen walked his horse toward the stable, his mind swirling and his body so alive that he scarcely could recall his business here at this big house outside New Market. The only thing that mattered was the young lady sitting on the porch at the front of the house, the raven-haired girl whose beauty and grace had shaken him to the core. She said she feared God; he knew his pulse raced and his senses quickened upon the first sight of her. He suspected his knees would give him little support when he dismounted to conduct his business. Why was he here anyway?

The horse on lead behind him hesitated. The rope in his hand tightened. *Oh yes. The horse.* He was to deliver the gift from Mr. Madox to his bride. That is, he was to deliver the horse to Mr. Phillip Roush, the father of the bride. What use *he* made of the animal afterwards was not his concern.

His concern was to meet—

"Rod," he muttered, "deliver the mare first."

The girl? He hoped the girl would occupy his attentions from here on, until his final breath.

He saw her in his mind, having memorized her entire being the moment he set eyes upon her. She was slight of body, but had curves in the appropriate places, and a face that had taken the breath from his lungs for several moments. When she looked up, he lost himself in her dark eyes. Her gaze stirred a tumult in his belly, and his mouth became roofed with sandpaper. He heard his mother's dying request echoing in his ears, and for that reason alone, he had uttered the words of the question uppermost in his brain, first surprising, then alarming himself. What had the girl thought?

Then he couldn't stop himself; she was working on what could only be a wedding outfit, after all, silken and shimmery. She might be Mr. Madox's intended. He had to know her status, her availability to become *his* bride. If she had indicated that she had an understanding with a man besides himself, with Madox or another, he knew it would have crushed the life out of him.

The slight, negative shake of her head in response to his questions filled his mind and body with such joy, such lightness, that he scarcely could keep himself in the saddle.

He had heard himself say impossible words: "You're free to marry me?" He was certainly daft.

Perversely insane. He almost thought the earth lurched and groaned at his ridiculous question. Surely he gave the girl occasion to think him crazed.

But incredibly, after a pause that lasted long, very long, too long, she had cleared her throat. She had run her tongue across her lips—oh, tender lips he yearned to touch, to capture beneath his own—and then she had set his world right with five words and her agreement to an introduction.

The matter won't end with an introduction, he vowed. *I will win her heart and her han—*

He noticed that his horse had stopped before the stable, and had probably been standing there for more than a moment or two. Also, a gentleman was striding toward him from the direction of the house.

"Soon, very soon, I will be in her company again," he said to himself as he swung down from his horse. Then he addressed the man standing before him. "Good day." He pulled off his hat. "Are you Mr. Roush?"

~*~*~

Julia almost fell down the stairs in her haste, but caught herself before she tumbled head over heels in total disarray. Now breathless, she took a moment to steady herself, then approached the kitchen door.

What had Camilla said? Her father probably was already outside talking to . . . that man. Mr. Owen. She said the name aloud. "Mister Owen." How well it sounded, as beautiful as the golden man himself. If Uncle Phillip was already engaged in his business with Mr. Owen, she could not approach him right now. But she had to know where her uncle was, what he was doing. She hurried to the kitchen, twisted the handle, and opened the door.

Cook stood at a large table in the center of the room, using two knives to cut lard into a bowl of flour to make crusts for the dinner pies. Julia paused to greet her before she passed. "Good afternoon."

"Afternoon, Miss."

The woman raised her eyebrows, probably in surprise at seeing someone invade her kitchen, but she did nothing to stop her, so Julia hurried over to the window overlooking the back yard and the outbuildings.

Yes, Uncle Phillip leaned over to where Mr. Owen held a back hoof of the horse between his limbs so Uncle Phillip could inspect it. Uncle nodded, and Mr. Owen—oh, how she wished she knew the man's Christian name! He dropped the hoof, disentangled himself from the horse, and stood erect.

Now they conversed.

Julia wrapped her arms around herself. Because Uncle Phillip was engaged in his business, she supposed she must speak to Aunt Susannah, but could not pull away from watching the men's interplay.

Mr. Owen gestured toward the front of the house. Uncle Phillip's gaze followed the man's hand. He looked back at Mr. Owen and raised his hands in a little motion that could mean anything, anything! Julia hoped against hope that he meant to say, "That lovely girl is my niece, Julia," but of course, he wouldn't say that. By now he barely knew she was present in all the hubbub surrounding Camilla's impending nuptials.

The men shook hands and Mr. Owen stepped back. Uncle Phillip evidently called a groom from the stable, for one appeared, took the lead rope of the horse, and walked away with the animal following him.

Uncle Phillip motioned with his head toward the kitchen, and Julia hastily stepped back from the window. What if they had seen her? Were they coming into the house? She linked her fingers together so tightly that they turned red. Surely not. But perhaps Uncle had invited Mr. Owen to refresh himself with a tumbler of water or a plate of cake and a cup of tea? Perhaps Uncle Phillip viewed Mr. Owen with more esteem than that of a mere servant. Were they coming into the house?

Her breath came in short, rapid bursts as the door opened. They *were* coming in. What would the men think when they saw her? Would they know she'd been spying on them? She turned her back, unable to bear the disgrace.

"Miss Julia, what you think of this dough?"

The cook's question surprised her, but she hurried over to look at the pie tins, lined up on the top of the table. The cook held out a scrap of rolled-out dough, and Julia took a look at it. It was dough, but the cook looked at her expectantly, eyes twinkling.

"Why, it looks fine, Hettie. You've done a fine job," she said, her voice sounding to her like she was strangling. "Fine work."

Cook nodded, her lips held in a tight line as though she pressed them together to keep from laughing. *She knows I'm spying on the men!* "Thank you," she whispered, and turned to leave the kitchen, but Uncle Phillip had seen her, and was approaching, his footfalls loud on the wooden floor.

"Ah, Julia," he said, and she knew she had to turn to acknowledge him, but she seemed frozen. Was Mr. Owen behind him?

Cook gave her a little nudge, and she inhaled until she thought her bosom would burst, then she turned slowly to face her uncle.

Yes, Mr. Owen stood beside Uncle, smiling as though catching a girl spying on him was the happiest occurrence of his day. Uncle Phillip also smiled. *I am in trouble.*

"Julia, I would like to present Mr. Roderick Owen of Mount Jackson. Mr. Owen, this is my niece, Julia Helm, of Cumberland County, Pennsylvania. My dear, Mr. Owen owns a farm outside the town and is well-known for his prowess with horses," Uncle Phillip added. There he stood, making a grand show of the introduction, but in the kitchen, not in the parlor.

This is my fault. I should not have come in here. If I'd been in the parlor, Uncle Phillip would have brought him there to find me, and this introduction would have been made in the proper place.

Julia raised her shoulders, unable to keep from the motion of self-protection. *No, no, no. You must be a lady.* With an effort, she relaxed her body, put out her hand, and amazingly, Mr. Owen took it, hesitated, then bent over it and bestowed a quick kiss upon her knuckles.

She wiggled her fingers loose from his grasp and clasped her hands together in front of her everyday striped skirt, wishing she had put on her best clothing this morning. But how was she to know this . . . encounter would take place, this meeting with a man she knew would change her life?

"I'm very pleased to make your acquaintance, Miss Helm," Mr. Owen, Roderick Owen, said. His voice had a warmth she had never heard before, an assurance, a strength that took away her breath.

But she had to make an answer, so she inhaled enough to do so, and said, "I am likewise pleased, Mr. Owen. Very pleased," she added, to her horror, conscious of the cook still standing behind her, soaking in her every word. She could almost see the amused expression on her face, almost hear the throaty chuckle.

Uncle Phillip, she could see, was enjoying himself, smiling and nodding and standing with his hands behind his back, rocking slightly to and fro from the balls of his feet to his heels, as though he had done something remarkable.

Julia lowered her head and stared at her hands. What now?

As though he had read her thoughts, Uncle Phillip said, "Come into the parlor, Mr. Owen. I'd like to hear more about your horse enterprise."

He forgot to invite me, Julia thought, as the men moved toward the inside door of the kitchen. But as he passed her, Mr. Owen grabbed one of her hands and tucked it into the crook of his elbow, thus ensuring that she was invited. In fact, his action came near to jerking her forward into an ungainly fall, but she recovered her balance, and gritting her teeth to stem her embarrassment, fell into step with him.

~*~*~

The parlor had no candles lit, nor was there a fire glowing on the hearth. Julia freed her hand from Mr. Owen's arm and hustled to a table where candles stood in holders, ready for service. She held her breath and struck a lucifer match, lit three candles, then took them to tables beside the comfortable upholstered chairs where Uncle Phillip and Mr. Owen had already taken seats. She hurried to the three tall windows, flung open the drapes on each, and turned to determine where she should sit.

The room contained several upholstered chairs and two sofas, arranged in one large part of the room, and straight-backed chairs along two walls for additional seating or to be drawn up to the main area, if needed. She could scarcely tug at one of them to boldly place herself beside Mr. Owen.

Uncle Phillip looked at her over his shoulder and pointed with the pipe he was filling to the sofa nearest him. Mr. Owen caught her eye and glanced at the chair nearest to his. Now what was she to do?

She decided that a third option—the other

sofa, which was midway between the two men but a little apart from them—was safest, so she approached it and sat, arranging her skirt with great care. This seat had the disadvantage of placing her away from the conversation, but she didn't care. She hadn't been invited here to discourse upon horses, anyway. She had willingly come because of Mr. Owen's action, and because she desired to be here above any other place in the world.

Because of his astonishing words to her upon their first meeting not even an hour ago—hardly a meeting, more like a chance encounter—she knew the man had an interest in her. She certainly had an interest in him, which had been awakened by his appearance and his assured manner, as well as by those unlikely words. However, she knew nothing of him beyond his name and his place of residence, which was, if she understood her geography correctly, several miles distant. And she knew that he dealt in horses. What else he did was still unknown. Whether or not he owned slaves was still in question.

She sat, and she listened, and she looked, made slightly uncomfortable that she had nothing to occupy her hands. At home, she was constantly busy, always occupied with one task or another. Being out of her element caused her heart to beat strongly against her ribs, and she feared that Mr. Owen could hear it.

He glanced her way from time to time, his gaze searing her soul as though he knew about her drumming heart, about all her faults, and especially that he knew she lacked experience in this less hurried world below the Mason-Dixon Line. He seemed not to care that she was such an imperfect creature, although she was acutely aware of her faults.

She was certain that Mr. Owen spoke to her uncle in deference to his position as the master of this house, but that he actually desired to converse with her, Julia. What did he wish to say to her? Would he speak again of marriage after such a short acquaintance, or would he attempt to learn more about her? Would he begin a lengthy, formal courtship? How would that happen? She lived so far away. What did men say to young ladies? She wished she had paid better attention to the conversations at Camilla's parties.

She became aware that neither man spoke. Instead, they sat in expectant silence, both looking at her. The heat of Mr. Owen's glance warmed her in an unfamiliar way, and her cheeks burned. Had one of them asked her a question? What could she answer? She had been off gathering wool instead of politely listening to their conversation.

Mr. Owen chuckled. "Miss Julia, would you

have any objection if I were to call upon you?"

He knew she had not been paying heed. He was amused at her discomfort and had laughed at her, blast him. She would wipe that silly smirk off his face.

She stood. "Yes."

His face went slack, all amusement fled. A look of dismay fixed itself upon his countenance. His assurance crumbled as though to ashes before her eyes.

Her chest tightened, burned like fire. *I have wounded him.* She sat, almost falling into her seat, as her knees refused to bear her up any longer. "That is to say, no. I have no objection," she heard herself say in a breathless voice. Knowing she had hurt him with her single spiteful word caused her heart to shrink, to collapse upon itself and beat with such pitiful action that she thought she would cease to exist.

How would she survive if she demeaned Roderick Owen, if she made him feel insignificant by a heedless word or deed? She must not play coquettish games with him, as Camilla was wont to do. Of that, she was sure. Doing such would destroy their tenuous relationship.

She watched as he gazed at her, unsure, unmanned, as though she had struck him a blow upon his heart. After a long, painful silence, she saw a transformation as it dawned on him that she had changed her mind, had given him leave to pay court to her. Little by little, he became a man again, regaining his confidence and his mettle, that verve that had drawn her to him in the first instance. He breathed, his chest expanded, and the afternoon sunshine shone its golden rays upon his face.

He squinted against the light, and then he said, "I'll be here on Sunday evening, Miss Julia, and I'll see you then."

Chapter 3

Once Mr. Owen had risen from his seat and left, and Uncle Phillip had gone about his day's business, Julia sat in the parlor, immobile. She could not find strength in her limbs to get to her feet, so she sat and pondered.

I know his Christian name!

That seemed the most important fact she had learned. That and where he lived, and that his business was horses. All else was immaterial. Except that he would return on Sunday. She could scarcely wait to see his lean face again, to hear the deep, velvet tones of his voice, to gaze into his blue eyes. *Ah, what magic!*

She longed to put her hands into the golden locks on his head, to run her fingers through the burnished strands.

Julia! She sat erect and her cheeks burned with shame at the feelings that swept through her body. Running her hands through his hair was an action that she imagined a wife would do, and she was not his wife. She hoped he had not had a wife. Brief jealousy roiled in her stomach, but she pushed it away as an unworthy emotion.

Despite her embarrassment at her powerful feelings, she ached to feel his arms around her, to hear his voice crooning her name in her ear. He said it in such a lovely way. With his drawling speech, it came out "Miz Julie." She liked that. It made her ordinary name extraordinary. It made her body vibrate.

I've never felt this way before. With a bit of difficulty, she shook off the shame and reveled in the peculiar sensations coursing through her. *Will I always feel like this when I think about Mr. Owen?* She hoped so. The sensations made her feel more alive than ever before in her life. She could hear insects buzzing in the hedge outside the window. She wanted to rise and dance around the room, but restrained herself in fear that Camilla or a servant would discover her.

She hugged herself, marveling at the new emotion, then it struck her that in the blink of an eye, she had developed an intense interest in a total stranger. But he did not seem a stranger any longer. Out of the blue, blue sky, the man had asked her to marry him, and bless her soul, she intended to do just that—if he did not own slaves.

A sobering thought came to mind. If she married Roderick Owen, she would not return home to Cumberland County. She would likely never see Jonathan again after her marriage. Did the angels or God know she would meet Mr.

Owen, that he would ask her to marry him? Perhaps that accounted for her strange fit of sadness when she had left her home. If she marri— no, *when* she married Mr. Owen, her home would be in Virginia. She would live in Shenandoah County. With *him*.

She sat in the silent parlor and for the first time in her life, she wondered about connubial relations. At the thought of spending time alone with Mr. Owen, the core of her being dissolved, like butter melting into the empty spaces of a hot biscuit.

She had no notion of what a man and wife did in their marriage bed. She had not known her mother, who died of hemorrhage shortly after Julia's birth, so she had never seen an example of matrimonial touch between her parents. But somehow, she knew that should she and Mr. Owen actually marry, his hands upon her flesh would be such a marvelous event that she might evaporate into the vapors of the night.

The only standard she had was the Biblical account of Adam and Eve. In the Book of Genesis, the Lord God had made a woman for Adam. She got up and found the passage in the Roush family Bible at the end of chapter two, then repeated the words of the last two verses in a whisper.

Therefore shall a man leave his father and his mother, and shall cleave unto his wife: and they shall be one flesh. And they were both naked, the man and his wife, and were not ashamed. Naked. She shivered.

She kept reading. In the next chapter, there was the to-do with the serpent, then God drove Adam and Eve out of the garden of Eden. She went back and re-read verse sixteen, for one phrase had burned into her mind: *thy desire shall be to thy husband.* Never mind the sorrow part, Eve was to *want* to be one flesh with Adam. Julia had no idea how that was accomplished.

She started chapter four. The beginning phrase, *And Adam knew Eve his wife; and she conceived,* sent such a hot rush of blood coursing through her, that she immediately put away the Bible and drew the drapes. She sat in the dark room, wondering about the "knowing." She suspected that it was a very intimate process, something that would bind her to her husband forever, and she very much wanted that husband to be Roderick Owen.

Is this feeling desire? Or is it lust, a sin? She could not quench the fire raging in her body. She did not want to extinguish it. She only wanted to see Roderick Owen again. She must see him very soon, before she burnt to an ember.

~*~*~

When Rod Owen entered his home in the twilight of that evening, he lit a lamp and went to a shelf he devoted to books. He pulled down a book of poetry he had purchased to improve his mind. He sat in his armchair, and thumbing through the volume, came upon the title, "She Walks in Beauty."

"Oh, she does, indeed," he muttered, and began to read, noting that the author was the lauded, but somewhat scandalous, English poet, Lord Byron.

He read the poem once, then again, and a third time he recited it aloud, barely needing to view the words as he did.

"She walks in beauty, like the night
Of cloudless climes and starry skies;
And all that's best of dark and bright
Meet in her aspect and her eyes;
Thus mellowed to that tender light
Which heaven to gaudy day denies.

"One shade the more, one ray the less,
Had half impaired the nameless grace
Which waves in every raven tress,
Or softly lightens o'er her face;
Where thoughts serenely sweet express,
How pure, how dear their dwelling-place.

"And on that cheek, and o'er that brow,
So soft, so calm, yet eloquent,
The smiles that win, the tints that glow,

But tell of days in goodness spent,
A mind at peace with all below,
A heart whose love is innocent!"

As he read, he imagined that each attribute resided in the person of Miss Julia Helm. He wondered how she looked in moonlight. He knew nothing of her beyond what he had gleaned from his very short interview with her at the porch, and later, their very brief conversation in the parlor. He thought she must spend her days doing good, for was she not here to assist in her cousin's wedding preparations? She had been working on the dress, after all. That exhausting labor had to be a good deed.

Despite his scanty knowledge of her true nature, he was very sure that Miss Julia—*his* Julie, as he now characterized her—was the embodiment of his dream wife, for the mere thought of her stirred such passion in him that he scarcely could sleep that night, and sleepily arose the next day to do his work, yearning for the next Sunday to come so he could see her again.

~*~*~

Sunday came at last.

A liveried butler ushered Rod into the parlor. Rod made his pleasantries to Mr. Roush and the fair Miss Julie, and was told to seat himself. He chose the chair nearest to the girl and sank onto the cushion.

One of Mr. Roush's slave women brought in a platter holding a pitcher of lemonade, glass tumblers, slices of apple pie already plated, and sliced cheese on a separate plate. Three forks lay to the side. The delicious scent of baked apples and cinnamon tweaked Rod's nose as she walked by and set the tray beside the girl he had come to court.

Julia did the amenities. When she handed Rod his plate, she whispered, "I baked the pie after church services. I hope it meets with your approval."

Rod took a bite and rolled his eyes in ecstasy. The crust was flaky, melting in his mouth. The sugary apple filling was perfectly spiced. *She can make an apple pie!*

When the woman had returned and cleared away the dishes, Rod inquired of Mr. Roush how the mare was faring. Mr. Roush inquired of Rod how the farm did. Rod noticed that Julia sat in silence as the men made their polite conversation.

Mr. Roush finally lit his pipe in signal that he had finished making small talk, and Rod turned to Julia to begin his courtship.

He conversed with her in low tones for some time, eventually learning the circumstances of her being an orphan except for a brother ten years her senior. He spoke of his own dead parents. Moonlight sifted through the partially closed draperies. Remembering Lord Byron's poem, he wondered again how she would look in the rays of the moon.

When he could no longer bear to waste the moonlight, he asked leave of Mr. Roush to take a turn around the flower garden at the side of the house with Miss Julia.

Mr. Roush gave his permission and rang for a maid to act as chaperone.

They left the parlor with the maid, who sat herself on a bench beside the parlor door and let Rod and Julia wander through the paths bordered with beds full of silver-lit blossoms.

"Are you acquainted with the poems of Lord Byron?" he asked, gently patting the hand he'd tucked into the crook of his elbow as they walked.

"I don't believe so," Julia answered.

He felt her shiver, but the evening was not yet chilly, so he did not fear for her health. He stopped strolling, let her hand loose from his arm and turned to look at her, positioning himself in such a way as to see her face under the tender light cast upon it by the soft moon. She raised her hand to her cheek. He sucked in a breath and stilled himself, not daring to stir lest his movement disturb the beauty of the sight.

At length, she lowered her arm. Recovering himself, he took both of her hands in his and began to recite the poem he had memorized during the past few days.

By the time he finished, he could see that the words had greatly affected her. Moisture glazed her eyes, which he hoped was a good sign.

"Is that how you see me?" she whispered.

"All the live-long day," he answered.

"I'm not going to pretend that my mind is 'at peace with all below.' It's been in a muddle since— since you brought the horse."

He had to strain to hear the last words Julia uttered, but they thrilled him. "I can think of nothing but you, Miss Julie. You invade my thoughts and inhabit my dreams. I even got bucked off a horse this week." He smiled at the lapse into reverie that had caused the mishap, enjoying the play of moonlight on her face.

She took in a sharp breath. "Are you injured?"

"No," he said softly, shaking his head to assure her of the fact. "Not my body. Only my pride."

She looked away, breathing rapidly, and he wondered if his mention of his body had caused her reaction. Polite folks didn't talk about bodies, but his yearning to marry her had ruled his thoughts all week.

"I don't know if I have a 'heart whose love is innocent,'" she murmured, and looked him full in the face.

He groaned, said, "Oh, my Julie," and pulled her into his arms.

The maid cleared her throat. Loudly.

"I beg your pardon," he said, letting Julia loose and stepping back. "I was overwrought."

She looked at him, her face wistful. "I cannot say I am displeased."

He gazed at her, soaking in her wondrous words, wishing he could take her in his arms again, but knowing the maid was watching. "You fill up the hole in my soul."

After a moment, she looked away, her face working as though she were dealing with an unpleasant thought. "My brother will come to take me home after Camilla's wedding."

"Are you saying you require a long courtship?" He held his breath, waiting for her answer.

Chapter 4

Julia left Mr. Owen standing in the path as she walked away several steps. Her heart pounded as she tried to formulate a way to ask the vital question that burned in her mind. *You're being silly, Julia. You have only to ask.* She took a few breaths to expand her courage, then turned and strode back to confront him.

"Do you own slaves?"

"No!"

She could tell from the clipped response that he had no intention of ever doing so, but she had to be sure.

"Do you aspire to own slaves someday?"

A look of annoyance, almost of anger, flashed across his face. "I work my farm myself. Someday I hope to have sons to help me, and a wife who will teach them that oppressing others is an act of deviltry."

Joy leaped from her breast into her throat. It filled her body so completely that it needed an outlet, and she was sure it must be shining through her eyes.

Mr. Owen's anger had softened, to gauge from

the look in his eyes. She put out her hand and laid it on his arm.

His arm jumped in reaction to her touch. She held on, although her own hand shook as though a lightning bolt had struck her.

Before she knew it, he held her lightly by the shoulders, and the lightning sparked still, a sharp tingling spreading down her arms and to her hands, which somehow lay upon his chest. His heart thundered underneath her palm, echoing her own.

"You will be my wife?" he asked, his voice choked.

She stared into his eyes, recalling the poem he had recited moments earlier. The words, the eloquent words—she lowered her eyelids for a moment—he had learned them for her, in her honor, to help him express how he felt about her. She wondered if a poetess somewhere in the world had written words equal to those, words that could tell him how she felt.

She opened her eyes, met his gaze, felt her soul melting again into a puddle. But even as she knew she had developed an abiding affection for Roderick Owen, she remembered the harsh truth. From now on, she would live far from the place in which she had grown up, the house she had so loved making into a home, a place of safety and calm. If only she had something from that home. She stood wrapped in melancholy for several moments, then it came to her.

She spoke in a rush before she could give in to doubt at asking an outlandish favor. "Will you bring me my father's chair?"

Mr. Owen's hands tightened. "Oh my Julie," he moaned, "anything you desire."

She gulped. She could not speak of her *desire*. At last she said, "I want something to remind me of my family."

"I reckon I understand." His voice sounded strangled. "Will you wed me?"

She closed her eyes and took a deep breath. Gathered herself together. Let out a sigh. "Yes."

"Tomorrow?"

Her eyes flew open. "I have no wedding dress."

He grinned. "I don't mind. I'd marry you naked."

She gasped. She choked. She fanned her hand in front of her face, remembering the Bible verse. After a moment, when she had recovered her wits, she said, "You are a perverse man, Roderick Owen, but yes, I will marry you as soon as it can be arranged."

He grinned at her. "You hang the sun and the moon, Julie Helm." He looked upward. "See it movin' across the sky, sheddin' a tender light." He looked at her. "You walk in beauty, my innocent girl."

He kissed her brow, then her nose, then her lips, gently.

She didn't mind at all, and ignored the maid's increasing protestations. The touch of his lips on hers had ignited another lightning bolt, and the fire melted her bones. In order to save her sanity, the sooner she could be his bride, the better.

~*~*~

Rod pulled back from a deeply satisfactory kiss and swore his heart was fluttering in a manner suitable for a maiden. Joy enveloped him, enlivening his nerves. He wondered if the servant girl now standing by the door—huffing her displeasure at him taking liberties with her charge, and probably some measure of fright, as well—was up for dancing a jig with him. He had to move, and he had no idea if his Julie danced. He looked at her dear face, glowing with happiness under the radiant moon. *She will be my wife as soon as may be.* Then he wondered what his next step had to be. He had flouted so many social niceties. Now he had to show respect for them and do things in order.

But quickly!

Ask for her hand.

Yes, that was the wise thing to do, even though he wasn't sure who should perform the office of giving her hand to him in marriage. Her brother was far away in Cumberland County,

Pennsylvania. However, Mr. Roush was close at hand, and he was her uncle. Surely he would do.

He realized that once more, her little hands lay upon his chest. He grasped them. "My dear Julie, I must approach your uncle. Will you stand beside me as I—" He paused to clear his throat of the emotion that nearly strangled him. "As I plead for your hand?"

"Now? Tonight?"

He nodded.

"Shouldn't you ask Jonathan?"

"Who is Jonathan?"

"My brother. He promised to be here in time for Camilla's marriage on May tenth."

"Two weeks away. I can't wait that long to ask. Things must be well in hand if we are to be married soon. Unless you're suggesting we run away, elope."

"If it can be arranged, I'd be pleased if I could marry you before Camilla's wedding." Her voice did not waver as Rod laughed and she continued. "But there will be no elopement. I want a proper ceremony, with a minister."

"Yes. That'll please the pious ghosts of my ancestors." He chuckled. "My mother threatened to bring them down on me to haunt my dreams if I didn't marry a God-fearing wife."

"She didn't!"

"On her death bed." He sobered. "I know I've

done much in haste, Julie, but I was smitten by your grace the moment I saw you. Knowing the situation better now, I can't bear the thought of you leaving." He motioned with his head toward the door. "The girl is having a conniption. Let's go inside and get permission to wed, so we don't scandalize the neighborhood."

She tugged one hand free and used it to muffle her laughter. When her mirth had subsided, she said, "As you wish," and giggled.

~*~*~

When Rod led Julia into the parlor, followed by the embarrassed maid servant, who escaped as soon as she could scuttle across the parlor rugs to the door, Uncle Phillip looked up from smoking his pipe beside the evening fire, and got to his feet.

"You've caught the contagion?" he asked Rod, then addressed Julia. "I'll get your aunt."

He departed, leaving Rod and Julia to stare at each other.

"What does he mean?" she whispered.

"I think he knows the situation."

"He can't have guessed!"

"It's plain as the nose on your face. You are a changed woman."

Julia put her fingers in front of her nose, and then lowered her hand to her side. "I'll have you know there's nothing wrong with my nose. It suits me."

"Nothing wrong at all," he said, shaking his head. "It's an adorable nose."

"Are you teasing me, Mr. Owen?"

"No."

"Well, see that you don't. I've endured enough of that from Jonathan."

He took her hand in his. "My Julie, I adore you. I adore your nose, and every part and parcel of you. Even the parts—. No. I'll save that speech for later. I won't borrow trouble tonight."

"Do you have a silver tongue, Mr. Owen?"

"A sil—"

"Are you trying to charm me?" It was too late for such attempts. She was already thoroughly bedazzled by the man.

"I often speak my opinions a mite too plainly," he answered, smiling broadly. "You will let me know when I am too plain-spoken?"

She smiled back at him and decided to try on a Southern word, see how it rolled off her tongue. "I reckon."

It tasted just fine.

The door opened, and Rod let Julia's hand loose. She couldn't help sighing at the loss of the warmth of his fingers as Uncle Phillip entered the room with Aunt Susannah close behind, bearing a somewhat puzzled expression.

"Julia, is it true?" asked her aunt.

"There, there, Suse. Let the young man have

his say. I presume you do have something to say?" he asked Mr. Owen.

~*~*~

Rod felt like a schoolboy called into the presence of the school master for misbehavior. He resisted the urge to shuffle his feet. "I do, sir," he finally got out. "I have asked Miss Julie if she will do me the honor of becoming my wife. She has agreed. May I have your permission, sir, to take her hand in wedlock?" He stumbled over the formal words, wondering if he appeared as foolish as he felt.

"Well now," Mr. Roush began, rising onto his toes. "You have slight acquaintance of my niece. What propels you to this haste?" He rocked back onto his heels.

Rod felt the blood drain from his face. The man was going to refuse.

"Sir, I am convinced of the suitability of our match, despite our short acquaintance." He felt lightheaded, and hasty words began to stumble over his tongue. "If we don't marry now, she'll soon be gone, and I can't bear to lose her."

The silence that followed seemed to stretch until his ears began to buzz. A black tunnel clouded his sight. His stomach appeared ready to betray him. Out of the haze, he heard a feminine voice.

"Julia, is this your wish?"

"With all my heart, Aunt." There was no denying the fervor in her voice. "Mr. Owen will treat me well, as I will treat him well in return. As he said, we are suitably matched, and I desire to marry him."

She had put emphasis on the word *desire*, and Rod felt the stirring of an equal emotion. He swallowed. Mr. and Mrs. Roush could not refuse such a passionate appeal.

"Will you at least wait to marry until my nephew arrives, to seek his approval as well?" Mr. Roush asked.

Rod felt a small hand creep into his. "Yes, please, Mr. Owen."

He glanced down. Julia was looking up at him, trusting him.

"I can wait a reasonable time."

"Then you may speak to our minister, Mr. Harris. My dear, will you wed here at home, or at the church?"

"This is a lovely room. It will fit all we need to have in attendance."

"Very well, my dear. Mr. Owen, I'll give you directions to the rectory. Mr. Harris is free on Tuesday evenings."

~*~*~

Jonathan arrived a week before Camilla's grand wedding was to take place. Needless to say, greeting her brother with the tidings that she had accepted the petition of a virtual stranger to marry him caused a furious turmoil in Julia's insides. But she put on a brave countenance and gave him the news almost before he had ceased hugging her.

"You're going to what?"

The look on her brother's face made Julia titter in nervousness. "He and I suit, dear brother. Besides, *one* of us has to marry, and you've made no attempts to get a wife, probably because of the impediment of having charge of a younger sister. Now you will be free to find your own happiness."

"You are happy, little Julia?" His face expressed his uneasiness, but also a hint of wistfulness.

"I am gloriously happy," she replied, and knew it showed.

"I must meet the man to judge if he can care for you properly." He went off to care for his horses, retrieve his belongings, and properly stow the wagon.

Feeling the power of having a suitor ask for her hand, Julia took it upon herself to send one of her uncle's servants down the road to Mr. Owen's farm to notify him of her brother's wish to meet him.

Scarcely before she knew it, Mr. Owen rode up the lane on a beautiful bay mare, which bore flecks of sweat upon its flanks. The manservant followed after some minutes, having no particular need to hurry on his return.

Julia hustled Mr. Owen into the house and toward the parlor.

He paused outside the door, straightened the coat he wore, and polished his boots on the backs of his trouser legs. "Do I look presentable?" he whispered, nerves evident in his wide eyes.

"You make a very handsome appearance," she whispered back. "Jonathan won't bite."

"We shall see," he said, clearing his throat. "Hold my hand, Julie."

"By no means."

"Are you fearful, too?"

She lowered her shoulders from their place close to her ears and threw them back. "Of course I am."

"What a pair we make," he said, and opened the door.

Chapter 5

The interview with Jonathan, which felt like he was being challenged to a duel by Julia's formidable brother, went about as well as could be expected, Rod mused as he jogged his horse toward New Market to see the minister. Of course the man had been surprised. Of course he had been on the defensive. Of course he had examined Rod closely, making much inquiry about his farm and his finances.

"I must have passed his tests. He did give me his permission," he told the mare. Now it was a matter of finding a day this week for his marriage, before the magnificent wedding of the cousin could take place.

He grinned at the thought of his Julie wanting to gently tweak the nose of the overbearing Camilla. He guessed that she would wear the mantle of complacence no longer. After all, *she* was *also* to be a bride. On short notice, but a bride nonetheless.

The warmth swirling in his soul made him laugh aloud as he came into the town. He was to be a bridegroom at last. He hoped his mother—

watching him from somewhere in the immortal realms above—was pleased with his choice. He thought his father would approve. Julia was impressively comely, but she was more than that. She had spunk.

A thought hit him. They would make beautiful sons and daughters together.

Before he could work that entrancing thought any longer, he arrived at the home of Mr. Harris.

~*~*~

Mr. Owen returned at twilight, grinning from ear to ear. Julia awaited him in the parlor, nervous as a cat with its tail too near a rocking chair in use. She sat alone. Jonathan had retired to his rest after his long journey, and the Roush family members were engaged in their own affairs.

He entered the room. "It's to be Tuesday."

Julia gave a gusty sigh as she rose. "At last." She allowed him a brief kiss, then pulled the bell rope to summon a servant as he seated himself on one of the sofas.

She told the girl, "Please inform my aunt that Mr. Owen is here and we wish to speak with her. If Miss Camilla is about, let her know she is included in the invitation."

"And Mr. Phillip?"

"Oh, of course, he must come, too." The girl departed. "Dratted nerves," Julia said. "My mind is a muddle. Uncle Phillip must be informed as well. It's his house."

"There is no need for nerves," Mr. Owen said, patting the sofa cushion next to him in bold invitation for her to sit beside him.

She did, snuggling against him for a moment, and then scooting aside. Just a bit.

"I will treat you well, as you told your aunt. We will begin our life together gently."

Julia's body tingled. Was he speaking of the "knowing" process?

"Mr. Harris said noon was a good time. Will that be agreeable with you?" His eyes shone.

"Noon is as good a time as any other to start a new life, Mr. Owen." She felt slightly faint. *On Tuesday I will be a bride. His bride.*

"The world can think of me as Mr. Owen," he said, and lifted her chin with his forefinger. "Won't you call me 'Rod' in private? That's how I am called by my friends. Certainly my wife should use my name also."

"Rod." She tried it on her tongue. "On Tuesday," she promised. "In private."

She was about to close her eyes to accept the kiss she saw coming when Camilla slammed the door open and hustled into the room. Julia leaned away, as did Mr. Owen.

"When do you plan to marry?" Camilla's harsh voice echoed through the room.

Julia stood and clasped her hands together at her waist, trying to stem the blush she felt rising along her neck. Behind her, Mr. Rod Owen got to his feet. "Are your parents coming?" she asked.

"They are coming." Camilla caught her lip between her teeth, then her ragged voice burst out again. "I asked you a question."

Julia let her lungs fill with air and her calm return before she spoke. "I will answer it when we are all together."

"You're becoming insufferable, Julia. Don't you know your place?"

"Of course. I'm your beloved cousin, come to visit and expecting to be treated well. Which you don't often do."

"Are you insulting me?"

"Am I? You would know."

Julia could not believe she was parrying with Camilla with such coolness. Knowing that Mr. Rod Owen esteemed her enough to offer her his hand and his life must have given her more courage than she usually possessed in situations with her relative. She smiled.

"What are you smiling about?" Camilla's voice rose in pitch as the door opened to permit Uncle Phillip and Aunt Susannah to enter. Camilla whirled about and implored her mother. "She won't answer me."

Aunt Susannah put her hand on Camilla's arm. "Calm yourself, Daughter. Your color is too high."

Camilla retreated across the room while everyone else took their seats except Mr. Owen.

Julia watched him a bit anxiously as *he* endeavored to calm himself. He held his arms behind his back and gripped his hands together. She wondered if she should be standing beside him.

He acknowledged her uncle and aunt with a nod. "Sir. Ma'am. I have made arrangements for Mr. Harris to perform a marriage ceremony for your niece, that is, Miss Julie, and me on Tuesday at noon. Will that be agreeable?"

Julia sensed that his knees were knocking together, then chided herself for thinking of his limbs. She could think of his limbs on Tuesday. After they were married. She felt herself quake.

Uncle Phillip turned to Aunt Susannah. "I believe that suits our schedule, does it not, my dear?"

Julia heard the rustle of skirts and looked up in time to see Camilla bearing down upon her.

She stopped in front of Mr. Owen, arms akimbo. "Tuesday? Do you mean *this* Tuesday? The day after tomorrow?"

"I do mean that day," he replied. Julia had a thrill of pride at the dignity in his voice.

"You cannot mean that," Camilla shouted. She turned on Julia. Rod moved as though to put himself between them. "You cannot marry before I do." She took a moment to stamp her foot. Actually stamp it, as though she were a two year old in the throes of a tantrum. "You cannot! *I* am to take first place!"

"Camilla!" Aunt Susannah rose and again reproved her daughter with a touch on the arm. "You must not speak to Julia that way. What will Mr. Owen think of your breeding?"

She rounded on her mother. "Mr. Owen? Who is he? Just a farmer!"

Uncle Phillip stood and joined the fray. "Camilla, you will go to your room until you can keep a civil tongue in your head."

As she left, Julia thought that the force of her scowl would have knocked a bull into the next county.

~*~*~

Tuesday came. Julia waited, peering out the window in the parlor until she caught sight of Mr. Rod Owen, seated in his farm wagon, driving a pair of horses up the lane and looking uncomfortable.

As he came into the parlor and saw Julia standing before the fireplace, wearing her Sunday best dress and a silk bonnet lent to her by Aunt Susannah, he inhaled hugely and smiled at last. In honor of the great occasion, he wore a pressed suit of clothes that fitted him handsomely.

Mr. Harris took charge, telling everyone where they were to stand. Jonathan stood alongside Rod. Camilla stood beside Julia, allegedly to act as her witness, but Julia suspected it was to make faces at her, instead. That was easily done. Her face was a study in wrath. Julia supposed that was in reaction to having her wedding supplanted by her little cousin's.

Mr. Harris opened the book he held and began the ceremony. He spoke at length on the duties of a husband and a wife under the rules of the church and of God. His voice rang with the confidence of his office. Julia wished he would move on and get to the vows. She so badly wanted to pledge herself to the man standing beside her, even though she didn't know much about him as yet. She knew enough. She had years ahead of her to learn everything about him. Her Rod.

Finally, the time came. Rod's voice shook a little as he gave his vows. In all fairness, her own voice quivered as she did the same.

As Mr. Harris pronounced that they were man and wife, Julia thought her heart would tear a hole through her ribs for beating so hard. She heard a sound from her brother, halfway between a grunt and a sigh.

Mr. Owen, her own Rod, looked at her with great affection shining in his eyes. He lifted her left hand and slipped a gold band onto her ring finger. She took in a quick breath. She was a married woman.

He took her face between his hands and inclined his head. He kissed her, gently at first, then with an increasing fervor. She felt his hands tremble. Or perhaps her face was trembling within them. Maybe they both trembled. It wasn't important, she decided, and lost herself in the sensation of his mouth devouring her lips as discreetly as possible in the circumstances. He lifted his head and she sighed at his retreat. She must find a way to do that again, and as soon as it could be done.

After the ceremony ended, Aunt Susannah hosted a small party, featuring Julia's ginger snaps and glasses of cold lemonade. As he tasted his first cookie, Rod's eyes opened wide, and a slow smile brightened his face. He caught Julia around the waist and brushed his lips over hers, leaving crumbs behind, then whispered in her ear, "They're very tasty."

She ran her tongue over her lips. So was he. She felt herself blushing at the thought that her husband's lips tasted delicious. Her insides quivered, because soon, very soon, she would go home with a tasty man, and she would submit to him, as Mr. Harris had said a wife was to do.

Swirling desire inherited from Mother Eve overpowered the quivers. Julia didn't dare eat anything, fearing that the heat inside her would burn to ashes anything she put into her mouth.

When she sensed that the party must end or she would become crazed, she hugged her aunt and uncle and thanked them for their many kindnesses to her. She touched cheeks briefly with a wooden Camilla, and embraced Jonathan.

"I will be well," she whispered.

"If not, Little Sister, I will come for you," he answered gruffly.

Julia ran up the stairs to the room that was no longer hers, changed her dress, collected her few belongings, including her recipe box, whispered to herself, "Mrs. Owen," and went back down the stairs, her heart thumping like a drum in a brass band.

Rod waited at the foot of the staircase. He took her belongings in one hand and her fingers in the other and escorted her outside into the yard as everyone except Camilla waved and shouted, "Goodbye. Good fortune."

Julia Owen smiled at her husband as he handed her up into the farm wagon. She mused that she was leaving the house in the same manner in which she had arrived. However, this time, she had a husband instead of a brother sitting beside her.

He lifted the lines, grinning at her like a crazy man—just as Jonathan had done—and slapped the horse's rumps with the leather strands. "Let's go home, Mrs. Owen."

Julia felt her insides heating toward a boiling intensity of feeling. She didn't know why it was happening, but she knew it was pleasant.

"How far away is it?" She would burst if the journey took much time.

"Too far," he muttered. "Several miles."

"Make haste, Mr. Owen. I think I'm going to melt into a puddle. You shall have to mop butter out of the crevices of this seat." Then her stomach growled. "Oh my. Pardon me," she said.

"You haven't eaten. I know just the thing to cure hunger rumbles." He grinned at her and snuck a kiss. "Virginia ash cakes. They're quick. They're hearty. They go well with butter." He chuckled.

It appeared that his nerves had steadied. She smiled tentatively at his joke. "You will have to write out the recipe for my collection."

"I plan to be too busy to deal with making such notes for you, Julie." His voice had deepened with emotion. "Observe how to make ash cakes for yourself. My hands will be otherwise occupied tonight than in writing out receipts." He placed his hand on her limb and she closed her eyes to better savor the heat rushing through her veins. She vaguely heard him say, "I adore all your parts, and I'm in a hurry to—"

She opened her eyes as he stopped talking. She looked at him. He looked at her.

"Julie, my heart is full to bursting with affection for you. My senses are more alive than ever they've been. You excite them. My body—" A wave of something that looked like pain passed across his face. "My body longs for you."

If not for the fact that *her* body was in an equal state of yearning, she would have been embarrassed by his frank declaration.

"Two more miles," he grunted, turning his face away.

~*~*~

Rod drove the interminably long miles to his home. *No, it's our home now.*

He practically raced through the task of putting up the horses. His heart thundered, for Julie stood waiting beside the door, as he had requested. His work done, he joined her and pulled her into a long embrace.

"My sweet Julie," he said, unlocking the door and pushing it open a bit with his foot. "There's a tradition." He scooped her up into his arms, nudged the door fully open, and crossed the threshold with her clinging to his neck.

He kissed her, then put her on her feet and said, "The ash cakes."

Then he knelt by the hearth and showed Julie how to form the simple cakes of ground corn and water, and cover them with ashes after nudging them onto the hottest part of the hearth to cook.

They sat opposite each other at the table as they ate the hot, slightly sooty cakes with butter and cold mugs of milk from the spring house. He could not take his eyes off her. She seemed equally entranced with him.

"I've eaten my fill," she announced.

He got to his feet so abruptly that his chair tumbled to the floor behind him. His heart raced in his chest. He took her hand. She looked at the floor, but followed where he led, to the room housing the bed covered by a colorful quilt.

"I am on fire." He drew her close.

She put her hands on his head and ran her fingers through his hair. She sighed. Or did she moan?

"How is it quenched?" she asked, her voice faint.

He swallowed hard. "I hope it never is," he managed to say, his voice husky.

~*~*~

The night was long and frenzied, and the fire was stoked instead of quenched.

Julia awoke to a raucous rooster's crow at dawn to find Rod propped up on his elbow, gazing at her. She felt wrung dry from the connubial activities of the dark hours, but summoned a tremulous smile and said the first thing that popped into her head. "Camilla must be livid with jealousy."

He laughed heartily. "Is that all I mean to you? A means to the end of annoying your spoiled cousin?"

Her smiled widened until she thought it would split her face. *You mean so much more than that to me.* She put her arms around his neck, intrigued by the way a lock of his golden hair fell over his brow.

"Rod Owen, you are my entire world." She moved closer and giggled. "I hope you found my parts to your satisfaction."

He groaned. "You're going to make the animals wait for their feed, aren't you?"

"I doubt they'll starve." She lowered her voice. "I do believe we suit admirably. I am the wife, the woman of Roderick Owen. You are my man."

"And ever will be," he agreed fervently. "Ever will be."

The End

Excerpt from
Gone for a Soldier

Rulon Owen hadn't intended that crisp Friday in April to be momentous.

In fact, when he'd saddled his horse in order to do an errand in Mount Jackson for his ma, he hadn't given much thought to anything but stealing a few moments to see Mary Hilbrands.

She was only a little bit of a thing, a girl with dark hair and eyes that shone like . . . well, they kind of smoldered nowadays whenever she looked his way. Those smoky dark eyes gave him a shaky feeling that spun his head in circles and tied his gut into knots that . . .

"Whew." Rulon realized he'd let the horse slow to a walk while he'd been off in a reverie, somewhere not in Shenandoah County, as far as he could tell. He got the horse loping again, and wished it was already a year from now. Mayhap folks wouldn't get their tails in a twist about them keeping company once Mary turned sixteen in May next year. He was almighty tired of Ben and Peter, and especially of Pa, accusing him of trying to rob the cradle because he'd taken such a shine to the girl. Yes. He'd concede that she was young, but when she spoke his name, his knees felt like they was composed of apple jelly.

Ma sides with me, he thought. *Pa was the true cradle-robber of the family when the two of them wed. Him twenty-four. Ma barely sixteen.*

He wasn't likely to throw his opinion on that subject in his father's face any day soon. Firm. Formidable. The entire county used those words to describe his father. Rulon shook his head. Receiving back-sass from his offspring did not sit well with Roderick Owen. But at age twenty, Rulon hadn't taken a licking for a long spell. *Maybe Pa's gone soft in his old age. That's likely, now that he has nigh onto forty-five years pressing him down.*

Rulon rode on, wondering what to do to get his father off his back on the subject of Mary Hilbrands. *It's time I ask Ma to say a word to Pa*, he determined at last. *She won't let him ride me once I begin to court Mary in earnest.*

He slowed the horse to a walk as he entered the town. Ahead, he spotted his brother Ben pulling sacks of grain out of a wagon parked in front of the mill where he'd taken employment over the winter. Glancing up, Ben saw Rulon, and stopped to raise his hand in greeting, a big grin splitting his face.

Rulon drew rein and halted. "Brother Ben." He clasped the outstretched hand. "What makes you so happy today?"

"I am put in a smiling mood from seein' you with that enraptured look on your face. Can't wait to thrust your hand into the cookie jar, huh?"

Rulon snorted at Ben's fancy.

Ben kept on talking his nonsense. "Oh yes, indeed. You're an enchanted man, spellbound and smitten, ready to do that girl's bidding."

"Speak for yourself, brother."

Ben laughed and said, "Give my best to Miss Mary," then smacked Rulon's horse on the rump, which caused it first to shy and then to run.

After a block atop the runaway, Rulon regained control of the animal. "Heartless boy," he grumbled, his face hot with humiliation. He settled the horse down to a sedate walk once again as he proceeded on his errand.

As he came in view of Mr. Hilbrands' store, he saw a crowd of excited men, some coming, and some going. Some were running. *Running!* What was amiss?

He drew up and dismounted. As soon as he had his feet on the ground, a friend of Pa's shoved the newspaper from Harrisonburg into his hands and bid him take it home. Slapping him on the back, the man ran down the street.

Rulon watched the man's hasty departure, then looked at the immense black headlines of the special edition. **WAR**. He read the subtitles interspersed with the text on the front page. **Ft. Sumter surrenders. Lincoln calls for troops. Via. Conv. votes to secede. Ratification vote in May. Counties raising Companies. Defend the Homeland.** His heart went cold at the urgency of the words. It soon rebounded, and began to beat at a rate he'd not experienced many times in his life. He looked up from the paper, his breath as quick as his heart rate, and made a decision. Feeling the cogs of his life shuddering to a halt and then changing direction, he strode into the store to put his plan into action. ∞

ABOUT THE AUTHOR

Marsha Ward writes authentic historical fiction set in 19th Century America, and contemporary romance. She was born in the sleepy little town of Phoenix, Arizona, in a simpler time. With plenty of room to roam among the chickens and citrus trees, Marsha enjoyed playing with neighborhood chums, but always had her imaginary friend, cowboy Johnny Rigger Prescott, at her side. Now she makes her home in a forest in the mountains of Arizona. She loves to hear from her readers.

Learn more about her fiction by visiting her website at www.marshaward.com